Pocahontas
the Peacemaker

First published in 2007 by
Franklin Watts
338 Euston Road
London
NW1 3BH

Franklin Watts Australia
Level 17/207 Kent Street
Sydney
NSW 2000

A CIP catalogue record for this book is available
from the British Library.

ISBN 978 0 7496 7080 1 (hbk)
ISBN 978 0 7496 7411 3 (pbk)

Series Editor: Melanie Palmer
Series Advisor: Dr Barrie Wade
Series Designer: Peter Scoulding

Printed in China

Franklin Watts is a division of
Hachette Children's Books.

For Bonnie Jo Hunt,
Oliver, Helena and Amelia – H.R.

Pocahontas
the Peacemaker

by Hilary Robinson and Masumi Furukawa

FRANKLIN WATTS

LONDON•SYDNEY

About this book
Some of the characters in this book are made up,
but the subject is based on real events in history.
Pocahontas (1595–1617) was born in a village in
Virginia, North America. She was the daughter of
Chief Powhaten, leader of the village. When some
English people arrived, they built a town called
Jamestown. It was named after the English King,
James I. Pocahontas visited the English people and
became friends with Captain John Smith. She helped
bring peace between the English and her people by
encouraging the trade of food, clothing and tools.
She later married an Englishman, John Rolfe. She lived
in England until 1617, when she died from illness.

The whole village celebrated when
a beautiful princess was born.
"We will call her Pocahontas,"
said her father, Chief Powhaten.

As she grew up, Pocahontas
helped the villagers with their jobs.
She made clay pots to carry water.

She watched the men build canoes.

When the hunters returned, she gathered firewood to cook fish and buffalo meat.

For many years, everyone lived peacefully. They farmed the land and shared big meals.

Life was quiet until ... the strangers arrived! They had sailed far across the sea, from a land called England.

The Chief was angry and shouted: "These people want to take our land. We won't let them stay!"

He sent his men to spy on the English and capture their leader, Captain James Smith.

Captain Smith was caught
and taken to Chief Powhaten.
"We come in peace. We want to
help you," promised the Captain.

"No," roared the Chief.

"You want to take our land,

then kill us with your guns!"

13

Captain Smith was forced to kneel down. The Chief's men raised their weapons. Pocahontas couldn't just watch anymore ...

She threw herself in front of
the Captain and begged:
"Stop! Father, he can help us!"
She began to cry.

The Chief was shocked. He dropped his spear. He had never seen Pocahontas look so upset.
"Please, Father, take pity!" she said.

The Chief stopped feeling angry.
"If my daughter wants the Captain
to live ... let him live," he said.

But life was not easy for the English.
The local people did not like them
living so close by.

Pocahontas knew she would have to work hard to keep the peace. "Perhaps we could all help each other," she thought.

The Chief still got angry at times.
He was ready to attack if the
English came near his village.

Pocahontas even risked her own life to meet the English, to warn them about her father.

Soon the English began to starve.
They did not know how to farm
the land and grow food.

Pocahontas wanted to help. She crept secretly through the forest, carrying food to Captain Smith.

The English were grateful and
called Pocahontas their angel.

They swapped their tools for fresh food and new clothes.

When Pocahontas returned home,
she went to see her father, saying:
"Look, they have brought us
presents from England."

The Chief was pleased and took the
English tools – but he did not know
how to use them!

Pochaontas laughed at the Chief. Then she had an idea. "Let's ask the English to show us how to use their tools."

The Chief did not want to ask for help. Then Pocahontas told him how bad the English were at farming. "We could help each other," she said.

So the English showed the
villagers how to use the tools.
In return, the villagers helped
them farm the land.

Years later, Captain Smith returned to England. He told Queen Anne, wife of King James I, all about Pocahontas the peacemaker.

Hopscotch has been specially designed to fit the requirements of the National Literacy Strategy. It offers real books by top authors and illustrators for children developing their reading skills. There are 49 Hopscotch stories to choose from:

* hardback